Farmyard Tales
Christmas

Heather Amery

Illustrated by Stephen Cartwright

Edited by Jenny Tyler

There is a little yellow duck to find on every double page.

It's Christmas Eve at Apple Tree Farm.
Mr. and Mrs. Boot and their children,
Poppy and Sam, are getting ready
for the big day.

There's lots to do for everyone,
including Ted who works on the farm.
Poppy and Sam are getting really
excited waiting for Santa to come.

Poppy has a new kitten called Ginger.
Naughty Ginger is hiding somewhere
in every picture. Poppy can't see him
but maybe you can.

Poppy and Sam have helped
Ted feed all the animals
and tuck them up
for the night.

Let's go home.

I'm cold.

Wait for me.

Now everyone is busy in the farmhouse.

They are all getting ready for Christmas Day.

Poppy and Sam run downstairs with their letters.

Poppy and Sam put on their coats and boots...

...and go outside.

Mr. Boot and Farmer Dray carry the tree inside.

It's bedtime for Poppy and Sam.

Poppy and Sam creep
up to the tree.

Mr. and Mrs. Boot
come downstairs.

First published in 2000 by Usborne Publishing Ltd. Usborne House, 83-85 Saffron Hill, London EC1N 8RT, England. www.usborne.com
Copyright © 2009, 2005, 2002, 2000 Usborne Publishing Ltd. The name Usborne and the device ♀☺are Trade Marks of Usborne Publishing Ltd.
All rights reserved. No part of this publication may be reproduced, stored in a retrieval system, or transmitted in any form
or by any means electronic, mechanical, photocopying, recording or otherwise, without prior permission of the publisher.
UE. First published in America in 2000.